Contents

Words that appear in **bold** are explained in the glossary

KW-483-084

The Mighty Mechanics

We are the **Mighty Mechanics.** Welcome to our **workshop**. We work on some amazing vehicles, and here are a few of the **tools** we use to fix them.

This is a wrench with a socket. It is used to tighten and undo nuts and bolts.

A set of screw drivers used with small screws.

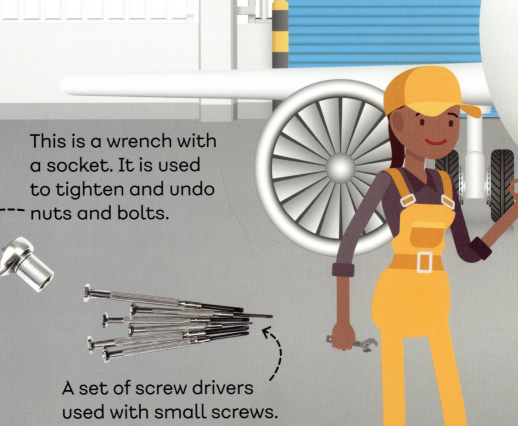

In the Air

John Allan

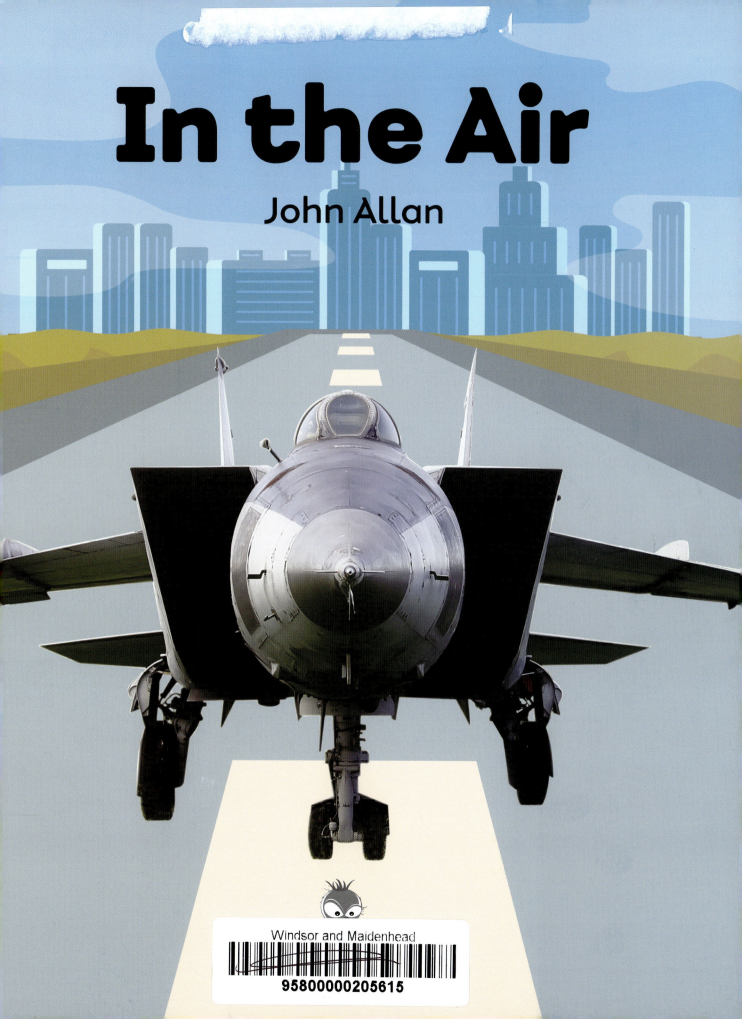

Copyright © 2022 Hungry Tomato Ltd

First published in Great Britain in 2022 by
Hungry Tomato Ltd
F1, Old Bakery Studios
Blewetts Wharf
Malpas Road, Truro
Cornwall, TR1 1QH, UK

A CIP catalogue record for this book is
available from the British Library

ISBN 978 1 913440 93 0

Printed and bound in China

Discover more at
www.hungrytomato.com

We often have to use a drill to make small holes.

Scramjet

Is it a plane or a rocket? **Scramjets** are a unique type of **jet engine** that have already reached **Mach** 9.6 in tests, and could reach Mach 15 in the future.

If travelling at Mach 15, a flight from New York, USA to Sydney, Australia would take less than an hour.

NASA believe that Scramjet technology is the future for space travel.

The first test model of an aircraft with a scramjet engine, the X-43A by NASA, was only 12 feet (3.7 metres) long.

Blackbird

The **Lockheed SR-71** (known as Blackbird) first flew in 1964 but it still holds the record as the fastest manned jet plane.

They flew at the edge of space so the pilots had to wear pressurised suits, like astronauts do.

These were top secret planes, operated by the United States Air Force and NASA.

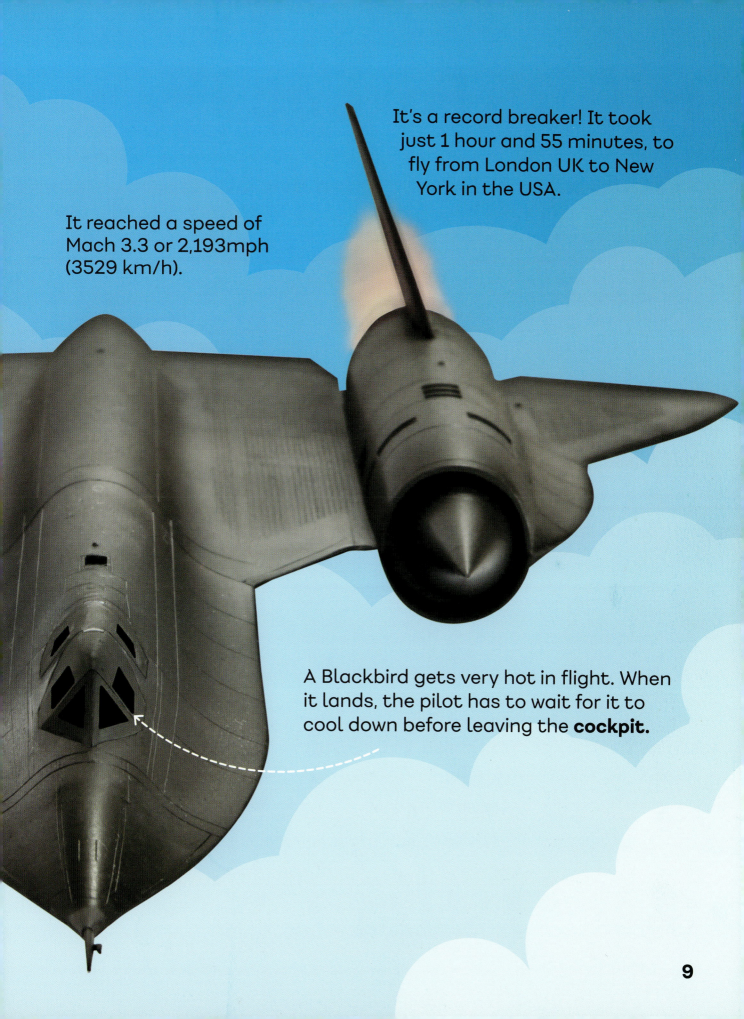

It's a record breaker! It took just 1 hour and 55 minutes, to fly from London UK to New York in the USA.

It reached a speed of Mach 3.3 or 2,193mph (3529 km/h).

A Blackbird gets very hot in flight. When it lands, the pilot has to wait for it to cool down before leaving the **cockpit.**

MiG 25 Foxbat

The **MiG 25 Foxbat** first flew over 50 years ago but is still one of the fastest ever fighter planes.

The MiG 25 was code-named Foxbat by **NATO.**

The MiG 25 is the latest MiG fighter plane, but is still not as fast as the MiG 25 Foxbat.

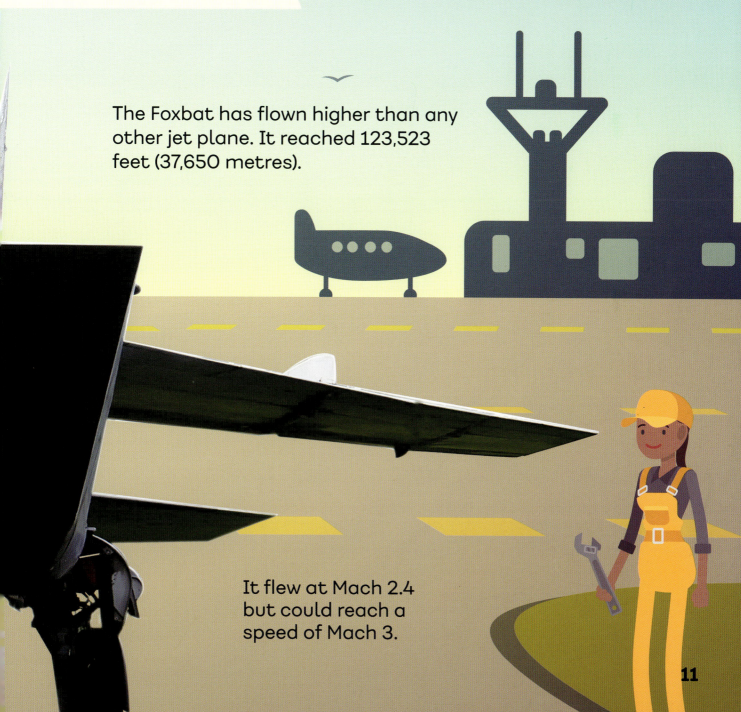

The Foxbat has flown higher than any other jet plane. It reached 123,523 feet (37,650 metres).

It flew at Mach 2.4 but could reach a speed of Mach 3.

The Spitfire

The **Spitfire** was very fast and **agile** and became the most famous **fighter aircraft** used by the British during World War II.

The fastest Spitfire flew at 450 mph (724 km/h).

These speedy planes were very good at avoiding danger and chasing down enemy aircraft.

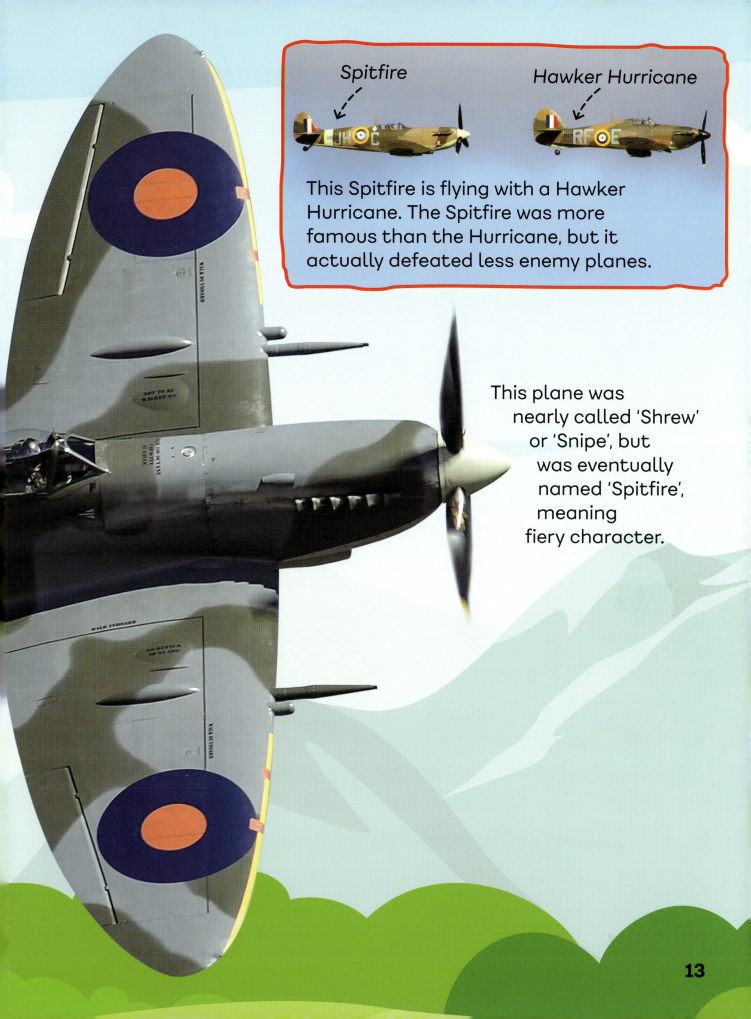

Spitfire   *Hawker Hurricane*

This Spitfire is flying with a Hawker Hurricane. The Spitfire was more famous than the Hurricane, but it actually defeated less enemy planes.

This plane was nearly called 'Shrew' or 'Snipe', but was eventually named 'Spitfire', meaning fiery character.

Wingsuits

Fabric between the arms and legs of a **wingsuit** act like a set of wings, allowing the wearer to fly a bit like a bird!

The fastest speed ever reached in a wingsuit is 225mph (363 km/h).

The wearer adjusts their flight path by moving their shoulders, and other parts of their body.

BASE jumpers, were the first to use wingsuits when jumping from high places.

The pilot releases a parachute from their backpack to land safely on the ground.

Red Bull Air Races

In this super-fast motorsport, pilots compete against the clock as they race their planes around a circuit with tight corners and **pylons**, called 'Air Gates'.

If any part of the plane touches an air gate they burst just like a balloon! The pilot would then receive a penalty from the competition judges.

The Zivko Edge is the fastest plane to compete, reaching speeds of 254 mph!

These planes are lighter than the lightest car in the world, making them very fast.

Apache Helicopter

The **Apache helicopter** is one of the most successful **attack helicopters** in history. It is also known as one of the most difficult aircraft to fly.

In the cockpit, two pilots sit in one behind the other.

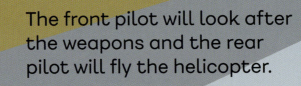

The front pilot will look after the weapons and the rear pilot will fly the helicopter.

In the USA, the Apache helicopters are flown by officers from the army.

The Apache can be flown safely in all types of weather.

This helicopter can fly at up to 227 mph (365 km/h).

Grumman F8F Bearcat

The **Grumman F8F Bearcat** was one of the fastest **piston engine** aircrafts. It was designed to fly from aircraft carriers during World War II.

Grumman built planes called Wildcat, Tomcat, Hellcat and Tigercat too!

The wings on a Bearcat can be folded, making them small enough to fit inside an aircraft carrier.

The Bearcat had a powerful engine and its top speed was 455 mph (732 km/h).

Pitts Special

These planes are specially designed for **aerobatics**. They are called **bi-planes** as they have two sets of wings.

The first Pitts aircraft were called "Stinkers" because they had a skunk painted on them.

In the USA, the Pitts aeroplanes have won more aerobatic competitions than any other plane.

They were designed for performing daring tricks, rather than for speed. They fly at 155 mph (250 km/h).

Glossary

aerobatics are spectacular feats of flying with loops and rolls, usually to entertain an audience.

agile to move quickly and easily.

BASE jump is a parachute jump from a fixed point, such as a high building, mountain and a bridge.

cockpit the compartment in an aircraft that holds the pilot and sometimes other crew.

mach is how fast someone is going compared to the speed of sound. Mach 1 is the speed of sound.

NATO is a group that represents 30 countries in Europe and North America. It exists to protect the countries involved.

pylon a tall tower-like structure.

Measuring Speed

A vehicle's speed is usually measured in either **miles per hour (mph)** or **kilometres per hour (km/h).**

1 mph = 1.6 km/h

Picture Credits
(abbreviations: t = top; b = bottom; m = middle; l = left; r = right; bg = background)

-= PHANTOM =- 1m, 10m; Amanita Silvicora 12bg; Andrew Rybalko (mechanics illustrations); Andrey Eremin 5bl; aShatilov 6bg, 16bg; Bas Rabeling 18m; DifferR 4bg; Fabio Imhoff 21tl; Golden Vector 22bg; Igor Kovalchuk 4bm; Jason Wells 19m; Joao Morais Almeida 2m, 17m; Julius Mason 13tl; Keith Tarrier 8m, 8b; Kev Gregory 20m; Lemberg Vector studio 20bg; Marc Ward 6m, 7t; MicroOne 2bg; osk1553 10bg; Razor527 15tr; Ryan Fletcher 22m, 23tl; Sean Pavone 4br; Soos Jozsef 17r; Stanislav Fosenbauer 12m; Tatiana Stulbo 1bg, 18bg, 24bg; Theus 8bg, 14bg; Tomi Mika 16m; vaalaa 11t; ViktorKozlov 14m.

Every effort has been made to trace the copyright holders and we apologise in advance for any unintentional omissions. We would be pleased to insert the appropriate acknowledgement in any subsequent edition of this publication